NO INSURANCE FOR A MIRACLE

SARAH LAMB

CONTENTS

To my mom, thank you for the great book title!

CHAPTER 1

Like he did every day, Stuart Pressman pulled on his boots and laced them. His blue scarf was wrapped a little too tightly and he loosened it before putting his jacket on over top. It was cold out, but it was also the kind of invigorating chill that he looked forward to. Opening the door, Stuart breathed in deeply. It was six weeks until Christmas. Soon, he'd be smelling fresh cut pine all over the Christmas tree farm. *His* Christmas tree farm.

Pressman's Tree Farm had been around for four generations now. There was a little pressure for him to keep it going, little being the size of Texas. If he didn't marry and have kids, his mother was fond of reminding him, it wouldn't continue on as a family business. Someone else would take over or it would fold.

While Stuart understood that, he hadn't found the right woman for him yet, and the constant reminders didn't help lessen the stress he felt over it. But that's how it went. Did he even need a girlfriend right now? He was sure one day he would, but there were many days he still felt anxious at the idea and turned down offers to meet this person or that. He'd been down that route, and it hadn't ended well.

"Probably not happening any time soon," Stuart mumbled as an unwelcome face floated in his mind and a memory took hold of him. "Maybe I do just fine on my own."

Yes, after that experience, he wasn't in a hurry one little bit. There was no rush to find someone and risk it being like before. Not even with family pressure to settle down. He needed a woman who understood his love of Christmas. One who would work with him to make the farm a success. Understand that the people who visited year after were like friends. Family almost. A woman who understood that he'd never be the richest of men, but she'd have his unconditional love.

Was that enough, though? Stuart paused and frowned. It hadn't been in the past. But that's what he had to offer. What he wasn't interested in was selling the farm, moving to a big city, and putting up an artificial tree next to a window overlooking the bustling crowd below, like she'd been hoping for.

This quiet life, the tree farm, small shops and everyone who knew everyone...that felt good to him. It felt right. Stuart knew that if he left and tried to be someone who he wasn't, it wouldn't go well for him or for her. But, of course, that meant right now he was lonely sometimes.

His grandfather assured him there was a person for everyone, including him. Someone who understood Christmas the same way their family did. But a woman like that was going to be hard to find. He'd just about given up. Truth be told, this time of year was just too busy to even be looking, so that was put on the back burner until later. He couldn't afford expensive gifts or vacations. There wasn't a lot in his bank account, and what he did have he was saving for a rainy day. Would it be possible to find anyone out there who understood and still respected the values he was raised with—hard work, no debt, and a spirit of serving others?

As he tightened his loose bootlace, he reflected further. Sure, life couldn't be like in a Christmas movie. Not everyone got a happy ending, he knew that, but it would be nice to have one just the same. And a little bit of wishing for something never hurt anyone. Sometimes wishes came true, both in movies and outside of them.

Ready for the day, Stuart jumped in his old truck, cranked the Christmas tunes, and took a slow drive along the graveled road that led to the section of trees he was opening to customers that year.

Pressman's Tree Farm followed what most Christmas tree farms did—rotating fields, and planting two trees for every one cut. However, the last two years had been dry, and led to stunted growth for the trees that were to be for next year and the year after. Hopefully, they'd recover and continue to grow steadily. In the meantime, he was counting on this field full of them, the best of the best, that had been growing for seven years.

Stuart pulled his truck to a stop, jumped out and set to inspecting the trees. He let out a satisfied whistle and grinned. It was going to be a good Christmas. In two weeks when he opened, the place would be packed with families hunting for the perfect tree. It made him proud to be able to give them that.

He roamed through the tall evergreens. There were Douglas firs, Fraser firs, white pines, Scotch pines, blue spruce...if he could grow it, it was there. It was important to have several varieties. It wasn't just about appealing to his customers and their varied preferences. His grandfather had taught him there was a practical side to it as well. Some insects attacked one or two types of trees but left others alone.

Grandfather had repeatedly warned him never to put all your eggs in one basket or your Christmas trees in one field. That's why they also owned four large fields, plotted into sections. They were numbered one through seven for the trees, and the last was the biggest lot, and where he'd set out wreaths, precut trees, and let a few local women bring out jams and jellies and baked goods for sale during the open hours.

It sure took a village to run the place, and his part-time help would be starting next week. Maybe he should hire a few people extra, Stuart thought as he finished his rounds and headed back to the truck. It was going to be a booming year. He could afford it with the number of trees he'd be selling.

The short drive back he thought furiously about who he could ask to come out and help. Some of the local teenagers maybe. He knew the women's shelter had a few. He could pay them, without them feeling like it was charity, but still provide the help he—and they—needed.

Hurrying into the house, Stuart settled in at his desk back at his home office and started making a list of what he wanted to do. Then he checked his order for the trees to replace what he was selling. They wouldn't ship yet, but he always liked to place it early. He created a simple sketch of how he wanted the set up in the empty lot, and made a few tweaks here and there.

A quick look at his email confirmed the tractor and wagon bed, along with hay, was scheduled for the customers to ride out to the field. The saws had been sharpened a few days ago. Not too sharp, but enough to do the job.

Everything looked in order. Stuart grinned as he closed his laptop, made a turkey and swiss sandwich, and let himself relax on the sofa. There wouldn't be much relaxing once the season started.

As *Miracle on 34th Street* played, he yawned. His head nodded, and he tried not to drift off. His own miracle was going to happen this year. He'd make enough to plant extra trees. Hire more permanent staff. Expand. Buy more land. Get repairs done. Really grow the family business. If he could do that, he'd be able to help more people. Give more Christmas cheer. Bring more smiles to faces.

His eyes heavy, Stuart gave into the sensation, and closed them for just a moment.

A wailing sound far in the distance startled him. Stuart looked around. The movie had ended at some point, and he was still on the worn out but comfortable sofa. The sound grew closer, and then he saw flickering red lights in the distance.

No. Not the distance. Right nearby.

Stuart grabbed his jacket and flung open his door. Was the little old woman who lived across the road in trouble? He should check on her.

The smell of smoke hit him full on in the face. His other neighbor, and the only other full-time employee, Carl, was running to him. His face was one of panic, and he was shouting something.

It took Stuart a full minute to understand what Carl was yelling, and then he grabbed onto the doorframe as the words sank in.

"The trees! The trees! They're on fire!"

CHAPTER 2

Allison Jackson had three cups of coffee—black, to match her mood—and the noise from a few cubicles over was still on her last nerve. "It's nowhere near Christmas yet. Do they have to be talking about it already?" she muttered, as talk of trees and recipes and wish lists filled her ears.

Jillian from accounting stuck her head in Allison's office. "Don't forget to sign up for the secret Santa!" she sang out, and then left again.

With a heavy sigh, Allison clicked a few times on her computer and put her name down for the secret Santa exchange. It wasn't that she wanted to. In fact, she could easily do without more hand lotion, a book she wasn't interested in, or a pair of fuzzy Christmas socks. However, she'd learned from experience if she didn't sign up, the others got downright nasty and whispered about her behind her back. It was important for appearances sake to get along with everyone.

She was also senior staff, which meant there were certain expectations. Including being the recipient of hand lotion, books she wouldn't read, and fuzzy Christmas socks. Luckily, there were also a few perks, being part of the senior staff. As head adjuster she had her own private office, and right now appreciated it incredibly. When things got too loud, or too Christmassy, she could simply close the door.

The office was little more than a large closet, really, but she took it. The building wasn't huge, and they all felt a little cramped at times.

A glance at the clock showed her it was time to get started for the day. She tapped her password into the computer and checked her company email. Her eyes landed on a newspaper article that the company had flagged and put in her inbox.

Pressman's Tree Farm in Flames! it read. Allison frowned. Where had she heard that before? "Pressman...Pressman... That sounds familiar."

Just then, there was a tap at the door. Her boss, Craig, stuck his head in. "Hey, we have a client coming in soon for an insurance claim. I need you to look into it."

"Me? Why me?" Allison wasn't the only adjuster there. Usually only the high-level cases came her way. Normal things, like a car accident or home break in, were handled by someone else.

She'd worked on those cases her first few years with the company, but her organizational skills had quickly moved her up in the ranks and set her apart. Now, at twenty-six, she was one of the top people in this location, and had gotten used to being more of a manger role than hands on.

"Read the news yet?" her boss asked. At her shrug, he continued, "It's the owner of Pressman's Tree

Farm. He's insured with us. The problem is that the fire department isn't sure yet if it's an accident. The word arson was thrown around."

"Arson?" Allison shook her head. "No owner is going to set his tree farm on fire. Not for the piddly kind of insurance he's got on it. I know I've sent him letters for a few years now telling him it's not enough." She tapped her computer monitor to show him. "He's got the bare minimum coverage."

Her boss nodded. "I know. But all suspicious claims need investigating. And that means this one. And that means the head adjuster. Who happens to be you."

"But–"

"No nuts, no buts, no coconuts," her boss said. "That's the rule. I've an allergy to all three."

Groaning internally and pressing her lips together, Allison nodded. As Craig left, she stood up. She was going to need something bracing to get through the day. Fishing in her purse for some quarters, she went to the employee breakroom, headed to the soda machine, and eyed her choices.

Finally settling, she pushed the button for a cola and looked in annoyance at the drink that had dropped. Grape soda? That's not what she wanted. Who even drank grape soda after the age of ten?

Still, she opened the tab, took a tiny sip and was pleasantly surprised as the fizzy bubbles burst and the fruity taste hit her tongue. Alright. Not bad. Maybe she'd try it again one day.

Allison headed back to her office and pulled up the Pressman Tree Farm policy on her laptop to go over it again. If the owner was coming in, she didn't want to be wasting time looking up the info. The sooner she helped him, the sooner he'd be gone, and so would the talk of Christmas trees.

Opening the file, she shook her head as the information pulled up. She'd not been lying earlier when she'd said that the coverage was at a minimum. The owner had ignored all their letters suggesting additional coverage. That wasn't a surprise—many people did that. However, it also put them at risk.

Most people would have higher coverage for something that was his or her livelihood. But not this guy. Must think nothing bad would ever happen to him. A lot of people thought that. Maybe he was cheap. That was another reason people didn't get the right coverage.

She snorted to herself as another thought came to mind. Nope, he owned a Christmas tree farm. That meant he probably had a Santa Claus complex. Denied himself to give it all to others. That had to be it.

She hated people like that. They were so fake. Such liars. No one really felt that way. It was all for show, just like when her parents—

A man approached her office, looking around hesitantly. "Excuse me," he said. "I'm looking for Allison Jackson?"

"That's me," she answered, and stood. "How can I help you?"

Allison took a moment to study the man. His eyes were red rimmed and bloodshot. He looked like he'd been through something upsetting. That, somehow, didn't affect his looks though. Tall, rugged, and good looking was the first thing that came to her mind. Light brown hair that was curling at his ears, dark eyes, and a perfectly shaped nose.

The man was stunning. How had she never noticed him around town? They didn't live in that large of a place. Most everyone knew everyone. But she sure would have remembered seeing this guy.

She mentally shook herself. What was she thinking? Why was she even admiring how he looked? Luckily, she didn't have to probe too deeply for an answer, because the man started talking.

"I'm Stuart Pressman. I'm here to see if I can get some help with an insurance policy that was taken out on our family Christmas tree farm years ago." He hesitated. "I admit, I don't know much about it. My grandfather took it out, and I just know it exists. I pay the bill each year."

An unexpected twinge of guilt went through Allison. She wasn't sure why. Usually, it didn't bother

her telling people they had no coverage. Or not enough. Or that it was denied. That was her job, and there were quite a few people who tried to commit fraud and others who thought by lying they could somehow get more out of the company, so she'd learned to treat everyone, and their insurance needs, as nothing but business.

But something about him, his posture, the look on his face, made her feel...sorry for him? That wasn't like her, and the feeling disturbed her. It was time to hurry and get this over with.

"Mr. Pressman," she began.

"Stuart, please," he interrupted.

"Stuart," she continued, "I've been looking at your policy. I was also just going over the fire marshal's report of the incident. Why don't you tell me, in your own words, what happened."

"I don't know," he said, rubbing a hand through his hair. Tiny curls wrapped around his fingers. "I had checked on the trees that day." His head shot up and he looked at her, a pleading expression on his face,

"The last two years had been bad, so little water, but I'd managed to keep the trees going. The water bill was through the roof, but the trees were alive.

"This year's trees were looking good. So good! Everything looked great. I inspected them, went back to my house, made a sandwich, watched a movie, and dozed off on the sofa. The sound of sirens woke me. When I ran outside, I could see the flashing red lights all around. A neighbor was shouting the trees were on fire."

Allison nodded as she took notes. Her keyboard clicked and clacked and she entered everything he was telling her into the computer. "Okay. What then?"

"I got in my truck and raced over. The trees..." his voice cracked, and her fingers hovered, but she didn't look away from the screen.

She was almost scared to see his face. But why? His pain was evident, raw. And it was making her feel uncomfortable.

"The trees were on fire. All of this year's trees. I don't know what happened." He was silent a long moment, his head dropped into his hands. His voice was low, and she had to strain to hear it. "Gone. All of it. This was going to be the year I'd be able to expand. Do more. Give more. Make things better. Make my family proud, bring a lot of happiness to people. Now, it's all gone."

She continued to make notes, then reread them to make sure nothing felt missing. As she came to the last word, there was a surprising pang of sympathy in Allison's chest. That wasn't something she was used to either. Not guilt and not sympathy. Not that uncomfortable feeling that she should do something to help. Could do something? Truthfully, few people's stories moved her. It was hard to feel sympathetic when someone ran a red light because they were putting on makeup and hurt another person, or set their garage and the neighbor's house on fire because they had bought illegal fireworks.

Sometimes, though, there were stories that kept her up at night, even if she'd never tell anyone that. Hopefully, this wouldn't be one of them. She took a deep breath, let it out slowly, and let the feeling dissipate. Calm, cool, business mode came over her, and she peeked at her reflection in the computer monitor to make sure her face was pleasant and blank. There. That was better. His eyes were focused on his lap. "Anything else?"

He looked up at her then, almost surprised. "I don't think so. They don't know how it started. At least, last night they didn't."

"That's why you are here," Allison said. "The fire marshal doesn't know if it was an accident or arson."

Stuart's posture went ridged. "Arson? I'd never do that."

"Perhaps not," she agreed, "but it's my job to go into all the details. And even if you didn't do it, it's possible someone else did."

He slumped back into his chair and whispered, "Who would even think about something so cruel? They are Christmas trees!"

Allison studied him for a moment. She didn't think he was guilty, but she had to do her job. She looked back to her computer and then felt her stomach clench. There was no choice. There wasn't anyone else. She was going to have to be the one to do it. To tell him about the policy. Why did she feel reluctant, though? She'd done this many times before. No big deal.

But this time it was. It felt different. And she really didn't like the fact that she kept having these feelings. This wasn't the sort of job you should experience emotions with. It wasn't a good idea. Allison took a breath and counted to five before she released it.

"Mr—ah, Stuart," she began. "Once the investigation into the fire is closed, we can issue you a check if the insurance company finds you were not at fault."

He nodded. "Thank you. Doesn't do me any good right now, but this way I can plan for the future at least. The trees are ruined. I've nothing to sell this year."

"You've a tree farm though," Allison said. She gestured around the room as if she could see it. "Don't you have thousands of trees? Does it matter which ones you sell this year?"

"I do have other fields with trees," he agreed, "but it takes seven or eight good years of growing for a tree to get large enough to sell. Those were this year's trees. The ones that weren't touched are pretty small. Not the size that typically sells. They have a lot of growing to do."

Allison pressed her lips together. A tree was a tree, as far as she was concerned. Big, little, they all got decorated, and presents got put underneath and, unless it was on a show or movie, someone usually ended up crying or shouting or getting upset. Christmas was a hotbed of emotions and drama.

The stuff in those shows and movies was fake. No one was really that happy at Christmas. It was all just an act. So, what did it matter what size tree there was? Put it on a box or something to raise it up. Better yet, save the environment and go buy an artificial one. It wasn't that big of a deal. The quality on them was better than it used to be, she heard. Some even looked real.

"...do you think?"

Allison jerked her head up. She'd been lost in her thoughts. Stupid Christmas. First it distracted others, and now her. "I apologize. Can you repeat that?"

"I said, do you think it will resolve quickly? I want to order replacement trees and replant as quickly as possible. Believe it or not, orders are already being made for new plantings, and sometimes there aren't saplings enough to go around. This is a prime example of the early bird getting the worm—or in this case, the tree species they want."

It was time to tell him. There was no other way. "Stuart," she said, lacing her fingers together and setting them on top of her desk. "I really don't know how to say this other than straight out. We will help you resolve this as soon as possible, but it's a little bit more than just writing a check after you are cleared of arson. Someone also needs to go and examine your property. You see, there appears to be some doubt as to if the area that caught fire is even under the insurance policy and eligible for the coverage."

CHAPTER 3

"What do you mean?" His voice was hardly a whisper. How could the property possibly not be under the policy? Stuart swallowed hard. He must have heard wrong. Clearing this throat, he said, "But...I pay the policy. Every year. I—I don't have my papers right now, but I can show proof that I do. That I own the land."

"Yes," Allison said, slowly. "You do."

There seemed to be almost no emotion on her face. Her eyes were fixed on his, but there was no expression in them. How could someone just sit there and deliver bad news like that without even a glimpse of sympathy on their face or compassion in their voice? He didn't understand. She was speaking as blandly as if they were talking about the weather.

He took a deep breath, hoping that he wasn't sweating, but his nerves felt shot right now and that was usually their first reaction. When the adjuster didn't say anything else, he asked, "So, how could I not be covered?"

She answered, her tone indicating she'd said the words many times before, "There are different coverages available for both business and land purposes available from our company." She motioned to a brochure, then handed him one when he didn't reach for it.

He took the offered paper and looked at it, but didn't really read it. His head nodded along as she spoke, but his mind felt numb.

Allison continued, "And it appears that the coverage on your farm is the minimum we offer and does not cover the entirety of the land. From this drawing included in your record, I can't determine if the plot that caught fire was under coverage.

"However, even if the damaged field is part of the policy, a payout is not going to cover your damages fully, even if it's proven to be an accident and able to be reimbursed by your policy."

His heart seemed to skip a beat, and his head felt light. A strange tingling filled his hands and arms and Stuart wondered for a moment if he was having a heart attack. How much stress could a person have in such a short period before such a thing happened? There was a crushing pain in his chest, but he wasn't sure if that was from the shock or something medically.

"...join you to access the damage with photographs for our own records," the adjuster said, and stood, closing her laptop. "Should we go now?"

Numbly, Stuart nodded and followed her out of the tiny office, watching as she shrugged on a warm jacket and reached into her purse for her keys. He hadn't heard all she'd said, but was hoping that he was doing the right thing by trailing behind her. If it was more bad news, he didn't have the desire right now to hear it.

"I'll follow you to the farm to take photos," she said. "It shouldn't take long, and I'll see how quickly we can get the claim processed."

His mouth had dried up, and the answer he tried to say didn't come out. At least he knew what was happening now. She was going with him to the farm to see what had happened for herself. It didn't seem to matter. He doubted that the insurance company would help, especially if this woman had anything to do with it. Even if they did, it wouldn't be enough to make much of a difference.

Allison was waiting at the door, a polite but bland expression on her face. It was obvious this was just a job to her. She didn't care. Why would she? It wasn't her livelihood that had blown up in her face. There was no resentment from him about that fact, just a sort of resignation. After all, what else could he feel?

Walking to his parking space, Stuart unlocked the door, climbed in, and clenched the steering wheel of his beat-up red truck. Several slow, steadying breaths hadn't helped. He just wanted a redo. A complete redo of the last twenty-four hours. There had to have been a way he could have stopped this. Changed the policy. Camped by the trees to protect them.

His eyes closed briefly, then he reopened them, started the engine, and looked out the window. The insurance adjuster was climbing into her car a few spaces away. He swallowed hard.

When he had stood outside of her office, he'd hoped she'd be nice. Understanding. Reasonable. She was pretty, with wavy brown hair, hazel eyes, and had a pleasant expression on her face...until he started talking. Then a look like she'd been sucking on a lemon appeared each time he said the word Christmas or tree.

At first, he thought maybe she didn't like Christmas, but who didn't? There was no way she was not the sort to like everyone's favorite holiday.

Now, he got the impression he was just wasting her time. That his policy wasn't worth enough or good enough to waste the company's time with. The thought made him angry. So did the fact that in the grand scheme of things, this was all his fault. It was his responsibility to go over things like insurance policies. He should have known that. Running a business wasn't just about taking care of the inventory, but all of the behind the scenes things too. If only he had done that, he might not be in this position.

It was too late for that now. There was no one to blame but him, and no one who would help him get through this, except for himself. Somehow, he'd need to figure it out. His business, his responsibility. That's what his dad had told him when he'd signed the property over.

Allison pulled next to him and rolled down the passenger window. "Lead the way," she said.

He nodded. "Right. It's not too far," he answered. "About twenty minutes." Allison nodded briskly and rolled up her window. Stuart sighed and steered onto the main road. The sooner he got this over with, the better.

The radio was silent. He didn't feel like Christmas cheer on the radio or anything else. Nothing was going to make this day go any better. He might as well just get it over with and try to salvage what he could of the situation. Not that there was anything to salvage. The fire had been pretty thorough.

When his truck eased onto his property a short time later, he stopped and got out. "We should walk to the field," he told Allison, who had also stopped.

"We can't drive there?" she asked.

"It's a mess from the firetrucks," Stuart explained. "Big ruts in the ground that are all muddy from the water they sprayed. We both might get stuck."

With a reluctant expression, she climbed out of her car and looked down at her shoes. Stuart followed her gaze to her petite feet and noticed the heels she wore. Ah. That was why she'd hoped to drive. Shoes like that were meant for work, not traipsing through a field.

"I've got a pair of boots you can borrow," he offered. "Might be a little big, but..." he stopped. Why did he offer? She wasn't going to want to do that.

"I'll be okay," she said, giving him a stiff smile. "Thanks, though."

Silently, the two started walking. Stuart made sure to go slowly so that she could keep up. It was a surprise to see she walked pretty well in those shoes, even if they were getting dirty. How did women do that? Naturally gifted in the balance department? He tripped pretty often over nothing.

Allison had pulled out her phone and was snapping photos as they went. "Can I ask you something?" she said, after she'd taken a wide shot of a cluster of trees in field three.

"Sure." Stuart jammed his hands into his flannel's pockets.

"Why Christmas trees? You could do anything else you wanted with this much land. Why trees? Work all year and only open for two months. If that. It seems like a lot of work, too, with very little reward. So, why? I bet this land would bring in a ton. It's a great spot for townhomes."

Stuart missed a step he was so surprised. Maybe he'd been right the first time. She hated Christmas. Who in the world would ask, "Why Christmas trees?" Everyone knew how important a Christmas tree was. Unless they didn't celebrate. And townhomes? Who looked around at acres and acres of Christmas trees and thought about townhomes?

He stopped and looked at her in confusion. When she paused, realizing he wasn't with her, she stopped too.

How was he going to reply? His mind scrambled for a coherent answer. "I...that is...this has been a family farm for generations," Stuart started, slowly. "Christmas is what we do. We bring joy to others by having the trees and wreaths for them to decorate with. This place is a part of hundreds of family's holiday traditions."

She shrugged then. "Traditions change. People can get a new one. They can go to a tree lot. Or a big box store and buy something they can reuse year after year.

Fresh trees are...well, forgive me, Stuart, I know it's your business, but they are wasteful."

"Not at all, if it's done right," Stuart insisted. He pointed to the field they were next to, where the four-year-old trees were. "You see, for each tree planted, I plant two or three more. So, they are specifically planted only for the purpose of becoming a Christmas tree."

"And then they get thrown away," Allison said, snapping a photo and starting to walk again.

He caught up quickly. "Some are," he agreed. "But the majority of trees are repurposed. Why, even Rockefeller Center's big tree is. Habitat for Humanity uses planks made from it for homes for people."

"That's a large tree though," she said, turning and facing him. "Not one of these, six or seven feet tall."

Stuart caught his breath as he stared into her face. Tiny lines were around her eyes and the corners of her lips. He'd seen those before, on his mother. She'd had them from laughing so often, however, in the case of Allison, he thought it was likely from her frowning.

"Well?" she asked, and then smirked. "See? A waste."

He shook his head. "Not at all. Trees can be turned into mulch, cut for firewood, used for landscaping borders, even arts and crafts. I've seen people make plaques and coasters and ornaments out of the wood. The branches are good winter insulation too, for garden beds."

He watched as Allison blinked a few times. "I guess you can reuse them," she said. "I'd never thought of those ways." She sniffed the air a few times. "It still smells strongly of smoke," she said, craning her neck to see further. "Are we almost there?"

Stuart grimaced. "It's bad in the field," he warned. "My eyes are still stinging from it. We aren't far away. Up this incline."

Allison followed, snapping a few more photos, then she sucked in her breath as they arrived at the field.

CHAPTER 4

A charred forest opened in front of her. Blackened stumps sat in a field of muddy trenches. Branches were snapped, their greenery burned off. The entire area stank of smoke and pine.

A quick glance at Stuart showed the raw pain on his face. It was obvious this tree farm was important to him, and the loss devastating. It was his business, after all. She might not understand it, and she didn't have to, but the hurt that was etched on his face cut her. She'd seen that expression before, in the mirror on every Christmas morning.

To cover her shaking hands, Allison snapped photos, walking around carefully. Her left shoe got stuck once, and she hopped on one foot, trying to recover it.

Stuart saw her struggle and jogged over, freeing her shoe from the mud and handing it to her. She accepted the shoe, and his arm for balancing. A warm zing went through her hand as she touched him and returned the shoe to her foot. Her heart started to do an unfamiliar speeding up. "Thanks," she said, glancing down first at his hand and then her feet, wincing. It would take a lot of effort to clean her shoes. Hopefully she could. This was a favorite pair.

"No problem," he answered, and stepped back as she released him.

It was only a second, a friendly gesture, but suddenly, to Allison's surprise, she felt a loss as they separated. She blinked a few times, unsure where that emotion had come from, and surveyed the field again.

"I'm sorry," she said. "It really is a total loss, as far as I can see." She glanced at Stuart, who was nodding, his Adam's apple bobbing as he sucked in a breath.

"Yep," he replied. Then he shook his head. "This here was the first field I planted when I took over the business. And now..." his voice grew soft, and ended in a whisper, "gone. Just gone. Seven years of hard work and dreams literally up in smoke."

Allison wasn't sure what to say. She felt uncomfortable. Maybe it was the way he was so open with his emotions right now, maybe she was just empathetic. She wasn't sure, but she was anxious to leave. Seeing things like this was her job. She needed to take photos, file paperwork, cut the check if approved, and that was it. There was no place for sympathy or getting to know someone. That muddled things, and could cost her job.

"Well," she said briskly, "I think I've enough photos. It does appear that this section is covered, according to the map that's attached to your file. I'll look for the updated report from the fire department and start on the paperwork as soon as I get back to the office."

"How long will it take, do you think?" he asked. "I know you said the insurance won't cover it all. But it's a start. And I'll be working on my end trying to figure out how to make up the rest, as well as pay my expenses for the next year until it's Christmas again." He gave a chuckle then, but it didn't sound very happy. "Who knows, maybe there'll be a Christmas miracle for me."

"Miracles aren't insured," Allison said, before she realized she was speaking. "And Christmas miracles only happen on TV."

He gave her an odd look. She recognized it though. It was the same one her coworkers often gave her this time of year, so it didn't bother her. Usually. Something about his, that almost hint of pity, made her press her lips together in annoyance.

She decided to ignore the irritation that started to fill her veins. "I've got your phone number, so I'll be in touch as soon as I hear something," she said, then turned to make her way back to her car. "I'm not sure when that will be, but I will make sure to follow up in a few days."

Stuart fell into step with her, silently. Though Allison wouldn't admit it, she was kind of glad that he was walking back with her. She wasn't quite sure of the way back to her car, and didn't relish the thought of wandering aimlessly through endless rows of Christmas trees.

Her eyes flicked toward him. He seemed lost in thought. As if he realized she was looking at him, Stuart looked over, and gave a forced smile. "I guess you are used to this kind of stuff, huh?" he asked.

"What kind?" she asked.

"Disasters. Personal ones, business ones. That life changing stuff that no one wants to have happen, like an accident or a fire."

She sucked in a breath. "Believe it or not," she told him, "you don't ever really get used to it, and each time it happens, you feel lucky that it wasn't to you."

Biting her lip, she stammered, "I don't mean that I'm not sorry, and I didn't mean to imply I wish it on anyone. I don't."

Stuart stepped over a large muddy rut. Her smaller legs had to take two steps to cross. Ugh. Her shoes were going to be a total loss, she just knew it. Stuart caught her eyes and said, "I understand. I don't think you are the sort to wish something like that on anyone. I just wish it hadn't happened. Not right now. This...this was going to be the year."

The emphasis he put on his words made her pause midstep. "The year for what?"

He stopped alongside of her and slowly studied the rows of small trees to their left. A wistful expression came over his face. "My grandfather passed away seven years ago," he told her. "That's when my dad passed the farm over to me. His health hasn't been the best, and I was glad to take over, give him a chance to rest. That year, I planted my first crop of trees."

With a bitter laugh, Stuart looked over his shoulder. "Those trees. They were going to be my first fully grown harvest. With them, they were going to not only give a whole lot of Christmas cheer to folks, they were going to pay for some much needed upgrades around here. Matter of fact, I was hoping that there'd even be enough to get myself a newer truck. Mine's a little over twenty years old, and the old girl works hard. I'd like to retire her, get something from this decade, if I can afford it."

He shook his head then, with a snort, "Won't be doing that anytime soon. But the thing that upsets me most isn't about the insurance policy."

"What is it then?" Allison asked, as they started walking again.

"It's the thought that I let folks down."

"Who?"

"My great-grandparents, who started this place," he said. "My grandparents—when I planted those first trees, I did it in Granddad's honor. My parents, who ran it for near twenty years. My customers, who depend on me. Most of all, myself."

Allison stared at him. She didn't mean to, but the guy was crazy. "This wasn't your fault," she said. Then quickly added, "Most likely. It's not like you tried to let anyone down. They are just trees," she said, "they grow. People will find another place to get their trees. Christmas will still come, and you'll recover. In a year or two, it will be like it never happened."

He shook his head then. "It's clear you don't understand," he told her. "Even if my customers get trees elsewhere, and remember me to come back the following year, that's not what matters. Christmas isn't just about trees, Allison. It's about making memories, and feeling happiness and joy."

They stopped beside her car and he gave her a long look. "It seems you don't know too much about those things," he said, his voice low. "So I guess you wouldn't understand, and that's why you just keep calling them trees."

With a nod of his head to her, he said, "Thanks for your help."

Before she could answer, he'd gotten into his truck and driven off, heading back into town, his words echoing in her head.

Allison pressed her lips together to hold back her anger. She understood plenty about Christmas and memories. They were one thing she'd never been able to get rid of.

CHAPTER 5

Stuart left the burger drive through and peered into his bag. The smell of the double burger and steaming fresh fries made his mouth water. He figured after the day he'd had, a treat would be nice. Tomorrow, it was eating cheap and cutting back however he could. There was a new field to replant, and no money to do it. Not to mention the entirety of next year to pay for.

The adjuster's words ate at him. *People will find another place to get their trees.* That was part of the problem, and while he wasn't ashamed to admit it, no businessman liked the idea of customers who had been coming for years leaving and going elsewhere.

Pressman's was a tradition for folks, and he didn't want to take that away from them. But how was he going to make it happen this year?

Sighing, he pulled up to his house, took his food inside, and set it on the low table in front of the TV. He hadn't told his parents yet. He didn't want them to worry, but he sure needed some ideas. Some help.

After he finished his meal, Stuart picked up the phone and called Carl, his employee. Carl knew what had happened, after all he'd been there that night, but he didn't know how things had turned out at the insurance office.

Impatiently, he waited for the other man to pick up, and when he did, Stuart said, "We've got to start thinking. The insurance payout isn't going to cover the cost. If they even give it. And we've got to keep the place going and the customers coming in this year, so we don't lose them, or the mortgage on the place."

In the background, he could hear Carl click off the TV to give his full attention. "Got any ideas?" the employee asked.

Stuart's shoulders slumped. "None," he said. "Except for selling next year's trees. But then, we run into the same issue next year, and the next. Smaller trees. We can't fully ever recover if we cut into next year's trees."

There was quiet, and Stuart could almost see Carl rubbing his long beard. "Maybe we can just sell half," he said.

"Then have half the customers," Stuart sighed.

"That is a problem," Carl said. The older man's voice brightened, "What about this insurance person? Is she pretty?"

"Pretty?" Stuart didn't see what that had to do about it. Grudgingly, he answered, "Yes, but she's also businesslike."

"So? What if you sweet talk her? Maybe she can do something more to help."

"It doesn't work that way," Stuart said. "Besides, that's not really appropriate."

"I'm just trying to help. Not like we have a lot of options," Carl grumbled.

"I know." Stuart let out a deep sigh. "Just...that's not who I am. And I don't think that's who she is. Anyway, you know I like to do things on the up and up. Get where I am through hard work. Not flirting."

"Yeah, yeah. But I tell you, it works for me. Wilma at the diner in town always refills my coffee quick when I wink at her."

Stuart stopped himself from laughing. "Isn't she just doing her job?" he asked. "Wilma's also nearing eighty," he reminded Carl. "And you are almost—"

"None of that," Carl interrupted. "Age is nothing but a number. Let me think on it. I don't know as I've got the answer, but someone might. I'll stop over tomorrow and look at the place with you. Might not be able to save the trees, but might be some that didn't fully burn that we can save the branches off of and make swags and wreaths. That's something."

"Good idea," Stuart said. A hint of a smile played on his face. Carl was particular about his age. He was up there though, and Stuart had known him since the man first started working for his grandfather. Stuart himself at been a teenager, so Carl must be his sixties now, maybe older.

Then he frowned at the idea of trying to flirt with Allison. He was so out of practice with women, it's likely she'd think he had some sort of spasm if he winked. He tried it out, looking at himself in the mirror. Oooff. No. No, that was pretty scary. Better not try that at all. Half his face rose while the other half crinkled. He creeped himself out, honestly.

"Still there?" Carl asked. "Don't be giving up. We have yet begun to fight."

"I'm here. Just thinking." He closed his eyes for a moment, wishing not for the first time it had all just been a bad dream. "Alright. Nothing can get done today. You think, I'll think, and we'll see what we can do. You are right, and I'm not planning to give up. See you tomorrow."

They hung up, and Stuart pulled himself up from the couch and headed to the shower. He just wanted his pajamas and a way to escape the events of the day. He paused, looking at the stack of Christmas DVDs on the shelf. Usually, this time of year he was watching one a night. Today, he just wasn't in the mood.

I'll bet it's because of that adjuster, he thought to himself. *She is devoid of any Christmas spirit.* "Must have rubbed off on me," he muttered. "That woman, I bet she's Scrooge in real life."

The thought made him chuckle. He wondered if she knew how sour her expressions were. How grumpy she seemed. He also wondered why he couldn't seem to stop thinking about her. As he flicked on the light in his closet, he chuckled again. "Scrooge," he said with a grin. "Fits her perfectly."

CHAPTER 6

"Well, Scrooge? How did it go?"

"I've asked you not to call me that," Allison said, as she dropped her purse onto the small table by her front door.

Her younger brother, Kenny, smirked as he crossed his arms and leaned against the kitchen doorway. "But it fits your personality to a tee," he teased. With a laugh, he said, "How is it, of all the people in the office you got stuck handling the Pressman Christmas Tree Farm case?"

"Darned if I know," Allison said, walking to the fridge and opening the door. She pulled out the iced tea, poured herself a glass and asked, "You want to take it over? Pretend you're me for the week? I'll owe you one."

"No way, not even if you owed me a hundred," Kenny said. "This is going to be fun to watch."

Allison didn't answer. An eye roll sufficed. She gave her younger brother a lot of those at times, but at the end of the day, she was kind of glad they shared an apartment. It was nice to come home to someone you could be yourself around.

Kenny worked for the same insurance company she did, but in the IT department. He got to work remotely, something she envied right now. She wasn't looking forward to work tomorrow, not with all the Christmas talk going around.

"I ordered pizza," Kenny said, "it'll be here in a few."

"Sounds good," Allison said. "I'm going to go change clothes."

Walking into her room, Allison kicked off her muddy heels and changed into an old t-shirt and pajama pants. Comfort was the thing she wanted right now for some reason.

She hadn't been kidding earlier when she told Stuart Pressman that you never really got used to people having losses, and the difficulty that sometimes she felt doing her job. It wasn't always easy telling someone their insurance policy wasn't going to pay out because of the fine print.

She'd done it many times and some were hard, no matter how well she hid it and pretended that it wasn't. For example, the woman whose husband let his life insurance lapse the month before he passed away. The man who thought he'd already filled out the paperwork for his new car's coverage the week before the accident. The family going through a hard time and didn't have enough coverage on their house the night the storm ripped off their roof. There wasn't much she'd not seen and dealt with. And it sure never got easier when there was a situation that was more than just an inconvenience, but life changing.

There was a look that always haunted her. She'd seen it many times—the look of someone desperate. Wondering what options were left. Panic. Fear. Desperation, just to name a few. She'd seen it all. Stuart himself had been wearing it today.

Sucking in a breath, Allison opened the door to her room, and was glad for the pizza to distract her. Stuart's face flashed before her, and guilt washed over her. Maybe she'd been a little harsh when she told him trees were just trees. It might be true, but she didn't have to say it when the man was obviously hurting. Sometimes she just blurted things out.

The TV was on, the news playing quietly in the background. Kenny already had the pizza box open and paper plates out. "Check it out," he said. "It's about the tree farm."

Allison sat on the sofa, lifted the slice of onion and mushroom pizza, and took a bite. A newswoman was bundled up against the evening chill, standing in the field. Blackened trees stood behind her. Stuart was there with her, an expression of complete loss on his face.

"Mr. Pressman," the newswoman said solemnly, "your family's tree farm has been a part of the community for over forty years. This is an incredible blow for you."

"Yes, it is," he answered. He took a breath and a forced smile came over his face. "But we are going to do all we can to be open and help the people who come here keep their traditions going."

"Forty years?" Allison said. "Wow."

"Yeah, they are a real staple of the community." Kenny looked at her with his eyebrows raised. "Don't you remember? We went there when we were kids after—"

"I don't," Allison said, her tone clipped. "You know I don't do Christmas."

"You've got to let it go, Al," her brother said, using the other nickname she hated. "What happened then happened. It's over. Everyone's moved on but you."

Allison took a slow breath. "We're not having this conversation," she told him. "Please."

Kenny glanced at her and shrugged, turning back to the TV. It was playing a dog food commercial. He jumped up. "Soda?" he asked as he went to the kitchen.

"I'm fine," Allison said.

Except she wasn't. Not really. She wasn't thirsty, but today had ripped the Band-Aid off of a wound she thought was healing, and tore it right back open. Kenny didn't need to keep rubbing salt into it. Sure, okay, everyone else had moved on but her. But had they really?

No matter what he said, she'd never be able to move past the hurt she felt when she thought about Christmas. Kenny had only been a little kid at the time. He couldn't remember how terrible it was.

As far as she was concerned, Christmas, and everything that came with it, was just a lot of fake smiles, a waste of money, and something that was an absolute evil necessity. Like the dentist. You suffered through it, because that was all you could do.

Kenny plopped down next to her, flicked through the TV stations, and settled on a game show.

"Make your guess," the game show host said, pointing at a fill in the blank puzzle that appeared on the screen. "What's the line say?"

"I can do without it," the contestant said proudly.

"Me too," Allison muttered, and rose from the sofa. "Me too."

CHAPTER 7

Dropping his head to his hands, Stuart let out a groan. Stacks of papers surrounded him on his kitchen table. Bills. More bills. Even more bills. All things he thought he'd be able to cover, but now he wasn't so sure.

There was also the stack of catalogues and website print outs he'd been browsing, dreaming about, over the last few months. His plans for expansion. His budget sheet for a newer truck. A list of upgrades he wanted to do and the costs of them. A better fertilizer and water irrigation system he hoped to implement. That wasn't even to mention his secret plans that he did each year. That was a non negotiable, and he'd need to find the money somewhere for that.

Pushing away from the table, Stuart grabbed his coat and headed to the field. Carl would be meeting him soon. Maybe together they'd make a plan. He didn't need to worry about the farm being taken away. He was close to getting the mortgage paid off, and his savings would take care of it for the next little while. But things would be tight—really tight—because something like this would take years to recover from, even if the next year or two was successful.

Still, he was serious about making it happen. No corner would be cut in his personal life, starting today, to squeeze a few extra pennies to put toward the farm. Tap water was cheap, and he'd be drinking a lot of it over the next year, only letting himself savor one cup of joe a day, and a single soda on Saturdays.

As crazy as it sounded, the night before he'd made a list of other things he could do to cut back here and there. For starters, five degrees cooler on the heat, and double sweaters. The savings probably weren't going to add up to a lot, but right now it didn't matter. His comfort for a year or two could be sacrificed. The dreams of four generations and the tree farm couldn't. This was his way of helping, until he found a new one.

Carl was already in the field inspecting the trees, bent over and looking at one. He turned to Stuart and raised a hand in welcome as he stood.

"Bad, isn't it?" Stuart said.

"It's not good, that's for sure," Carl answered, "but trees can be replaced. People and photographs can't be. I'll bet you're real glad it wasn't the house instead."

"Sure am," Stuart said. He'd thought about that a lot over the last twenty-four hours.

His house was one his grandfather had built with his great grandfather's help decades ago. That would have been irreplaceable. The single-story home might not be worth a lot money wise, but to him, it was where every Christmas was spent, and a whole lot of summers and falls, working with the trees. There were sure a lot of memories there.

Stuart glanced at Carl. The other man was walking around, looking at the burned stumps, charred branches, and torn up ground. "Any ideas?" he asked. "I won't lie. I've got none, other than selling a portion of the smaller trees, and praying that the rest grow fast."

Carl nodded. "I'm afraid that's all I've got too. You could sell half of field six, and then go and cut maybe ten percent of field five for small precuts. I can trim the bottoms and we can swag and wreath the branches like usual. Just means a smaller harvest this year. I'm sure folks will understand though. You'll still have plenty coming out to support you. The problem then becomes the question of will you have enough trees, and then what will you do next year, again with only half as many trees to sell. They can't grow fast enough to get caught up."

"You are right, the customers will come," Stuart agreed. "But somehow, selling less and selling smaller doesn't feel right. It feels like giving up."

"What do you want to do then?" Carl asked. He crossed his arms over his chest. "There's not much stock. I reckon I could ask a few of the other farms, see if they'd cut a discount to let you have some of their inventory."

Stuart thought about that idea for a moment. He could do that. Maybe some of them would be willing. A dozen trees here, a dozen trees there...but would they? And why would they sell them for less when they could get their full price? Still, it was something to consider. If the situation was reversed, he knew he'd be helping them. Maybe the same would be true on their end.

"Okay," he said. "Would you make a few calls? See what they say? It's not a yes, so don't make a firm commitment, but it's an avenue to explore."

Carl nodded. "Won't lie, Stuart. I'm not feeling really optimistic about that idea, but we are up against the wall and don't have much available to us. Sure hope that gal with the insurance company pulls through with a miracle. Remember what I said. Don't forget to wink at her a few times. See if that helps."

Stuart scoffed and surveyed the field of ruin, as he shook his head slowly. "Winking a few times isn't going to fix this, old man. I've a feeling nothing but hard work and time will." The usual excitement and hope and joy in his heart this time of year had vanished. All that remained was a depressed feeling that he didn't recall ever having, and sure didn't like experiencing.

It wasn't about the hard work. That wasn't something he ever minded doing. He enjoyed the satisfaction of a job well done. It just was this wasn't something that hard work alone could take care of. Time was needed too, and that was not something he had enough of to fix things before Christmas.

For a moment, he closed his eyes. If this was a movie or a book, right about now this would be the dark point. The time when it just didn't feel like there was a chance. But then something would happen to turn things around. Make it all right. Save the farm.

"Don't give up. It's not the time of year for that. It's going to work out, and better than you hope," Carl said, and rested a hand on Stuart's shoulder.

Stuart's thoughts flitted to the insurance adjuster. Allison. Something she said came to mind at the old man's words and he grimaced as he looked at Carl. "I doubt it. As she told me, there's no insurance for a miracle."

CHAPTER 8

Allison hurried into the office. She was never late, but today was an exception. Luckily, no one said anything. Everyone tended to give grace for that sort of thing if it wasn't a frequent occurrence, and with her, it never was.

Dropping her purse onto her desk, she headed to the breakroom fridge to drop off her lunch and make a coffee. Chatter filled the office today, more than usual. As she let herself listen curiously, it surprised her. Everything seemed to be focused on a single topic. The Pressman tree farm.

"...since we were kids."

"Wouldn't feel right getting my tree elsewhere. But I don't even know if he will have them."

"...a tradition the kids always look forward to."

"Favorite thing to do that weekend."

"We always go with my in-laws, then visit the diner afterward."

Allison weaved her way through the building back to her office. She was near it when Craig stopped her. "How's it going on the Pressman case?" he asked.

It felt like every eye in the room was on her. It was an uncomfortable, prickling sensation, like she'd had back in high school when she, the unpopular girl, had walked into the wrong classroom by mistake. She half expected the laughter to start. Instead, she was surprised her quick glimpse showed tense faces. Concern.

"I don't have any follow up yet from the fire marshal," she said. "From what I personally saw, it wasn't intentional and the affected field is under the policy, so his policy will cover part of the loss."

"Only part?" a coworker asked. "Why only part?"

"He didn't have a large enough policy," Allison said.

"Oh wow. I wonder what will happen," the coworker said. "It's not Christmas without that place. Maybe the town can take up a collection."

"Keep me updated," Craig said, turning to leave. "What that man needs is a miracle."

"It's that time of year," Flora, the receptionist, said. "Maybe it will happen."

At the chorus of "yes" and "amen" Allison looked up in surprise. She hadn't realized nearly everyone in the office, including a few clients, were listening in, but there they were, nodding in agreement.

"Miracles don't happen like that," Allison said.

"They can and they do," Flora said firmly.

Allison didn't answer, but made her way back to her office and closed the door. Taking a deep breath, she rested her head on her hands for a moment.

"It's not true, you know," she said to the tiny penguin that sat near her office phone. Kenny had given it to her for her birthday. For some reason, though it was an odd gift, she liked it.

Reaching over, she adjusted the penguin and met his eyes. "Miracles don't always happen this time of year." Her lips pressed together. "Not for me, anyway."

Opening her email, she scanned what had arrived. Nothing related to the Pressman tree farm. Her phone rang, and she saw it was her mom. Surprised, she picked up the phone.

"Hey Mom, you okay?"

"Of course," her mother's voice came through. "I'm fine! But are you?"

"Me?" Allison swallowed. How did her mother do that? She always seemed to know when something was upsetting her.

"Yes, you." Her mother waited, and the line crackled in the silence.

Had Kenny been talking to her? Allison wondered, but then rejected the thought. No, Kenny didn't worry about stuff like that. She smiled, hoping her voice carried a hint of it so her mom wouldn't be worried. "I'm good. Just working on a heavy insurance case right now."

"I hope not too terrible," her mother said.

Allison wound the old-fashioned phone cord around her finger, letting it coil around her. "It's for the Pressman Christmas tree farm."

The gasp that came through the phone nearly terrified Allison into thinking something was wrong with her mother, until she exclaimed, "Not the Pressman farm! I saw that on the news."

"It made the news up there?" Allison asked. "You are like four states away."

"It did," her mother agreed. "Oh, the good times we had at that place when you were growing up."

Allison blinked. "You mean...that's where we went to get our trees?"

"It was," her mother said. "Until—"

"Stop," Allison said. "I already know what happened. I don't need to relive it." She pressed her lips together, then offered, "I'm sorry. It's just..."

There was a long stretch of silence. She couldn't continue, and so just waited for her mother to resume the conversation. When she didn't, Allison checked to see if the phone had disconnected. Finally, she heard her mother sigh. "I know Christmas, and trees in particular, bring up a lot of bad memories for you. How are you handling this?"

"Just fine," Allison said. "It's a typical day at the office."

"Mm," her mother said in that way she always did when she didn't believe her, but wasn't going to contradict what she said.

"Everyone at the office seems a little upset," Allison said.

"I'm sure. That place is very important to a lot of people. It's a huge part of their traditions."

"That's what Stuart said," Allison mused.

"Stuart? Who's Stuart?" her mother asked, perking right up.

"Stuart Pressman," Allison said.

"Ohhhh. And is Stuart handsome?" her mother asked.

"Mom! He's a client. Not a date," Allison said.

"Mmmhmmm."

To Allison's horror, and to her surprise, she was blushing. She pressed a hand to one cheek. Why was it so warm? She had zero interest in Christmas tree man. He reeked of Christmas spirit, and she ran the opposite way of it. They weren't compatible at all.

Her mother's voice broke over the phone, "Well, who knows. Maybe something good will come out of this."

"How so?" Allison asked. That was another thing her mom did, always look for the bright side.

"Like a phoenix rising from the ashes," came the reply. "Or a small town Christmas miracle."

"You sound as sappy as everyone else I work with," Allison groaned. "What is it with everyone and Christmas miracles? They're just a bunch of junk. They don't exist."

Her mother was silent, and Allison could feel the weight over the phone of her mother's sorrow. "Allison, for you, no. There wasn't a Christmas miracle like you wanted and hoped for. But there was a miracle. We all escaped the house fire. No one was hurt. Things worked out. It was difficult for a while, but we got through. We were lucky, when you think about it."

"Yeah, well, where was our Christmas Day miracle, Mom?" Allison asked, the heat in her voice still there from that terrible Christmas. "Where were the people rushing in to help us? To replace our toys, our tree, our memories? Helping us when we were stuck in that crummy motel, crammed together like sardines? To take away that feeling of being helpless and scared? We didn't get that. In fact, it's like everyone forgot about us and that we were struggling and scared. Real, not TV or movie miracles at Christmas where everything suddenly is okay? They just don't exist. We'd all be a lot better off without Christmas. Who needs decorated trees? And why should you give gifts to those you love only one day of the year?"

Allison's chest was rising and falling rapidly. She hated Christmas. That morning of the fire, neighbors had stood around staring at them in shock. But no one had offered help. She stood shivering in her thin nightgown and crying, while everyone just watched and pointed. The firemen came and put out the flames, the neighbors had turned back to their homes and their festivities, and her family had stood looking at a smoke filled, water damaged mess.

There were no gifts. There was no tree. There was no television, or games, or books. All of it had gone up in flames when the strand of lights on the tree malfunctioned and caught the branches on fire.

Sure, they'd gotten out okay. And yeah, that was a miracle, she guessed, but to a child of eleven, one who'd spent year after year devouring Christmas movies where there was always a happy ending, where everyone helped and loved, and laughed and every Christmas was filled with magic and hope...she felt incredibly let down. None of that had happened for them. Why? Her little mind had grappled with that question for weeks after. Eventually, she'd come to the conclusion that Christmas miracles were just fake.

"Sometimes," her mother said slowly, "even if things are different and not what we want, it's about coming together with a new idea that makes everything right."

Allison sat with that thought. Then she threw it away. Her mother was wrong. "That's not what traditions are," she said quietly. "They are something that happen year after year and never change."

"But without that change," her mother said gently, "there's not a chance for something better."

A ping in her email inbox made her look over. An excuse to end the call was welcome. "Mom, I've got to go. The fire marshal's report on the tree farm came in. I've got to get working on it,"

"Alright," her mother said. Then she added, "But Allison, please remember what I said. And don't be so quick to discard the traditions and joy that others have, just because you don't want it for yourself."

"Mmhmm," Allison said, not really paying attention as she clicked on the email. The sooner this got resolved, the sooner she could stop worrying about it. With any luck, it would be today. She sure hoped so.

"And maybe ask that cute guy out for coffee. I hate you being alone. Stuart is such a nice name! I would love a son-in-law with that name."

"Bye, Mom. Love you."

The call disconnected and Allison skimmed the report, then carefully started at the beginning to read it. When she got to the end, she let out a long sigh.

Tapping her fingers over the laptop's keyboard, she opened up Stuart's account, located his phone number and punched it in on her desk phone. She finally had news, which also meant the days of his open file were numbered.

Hopefully soon she could forget about Christmas—and all the terrible memories associated with it.

CHAPTER 9

His phone was ringing in his back pocket, but Stuart ignored it. He dragged another burned tree to the trailer that was usually used for hauling guests and their trees to and from the entrance. He and Carl had decided to just clear the field completely. Out of sight, out of mind. That and it was a total loss.

It had been several days since the adjuster had been out and taken photos. He wondered how the process was going. Truth be told, he'd been too busy to ask many questions about the timeline or even call her, but her face kept popping into his mind more than he'd care to admit.

He found himself wondering what Allison would look like if she smiled more. And what it would take to put that smile there. He bet it would light up her face, and those tiny lines by her eyes would crinkle with joy.

Stuart let out a grunt as he sawed down another stump. This was exhausting work, but it had to be done. It wasn't like he could do anything with the mess still in the field. However, if they cleared it all out, since there was nothing worth salvaging, it would be ready for replanting as soon as possible.

There was another important reason to get it all done quickly. Inevitably, there would be customers to the tree farm who wanted to wander around and see the damage. Even if the field were roped off, someone would sneak in, there was no doubt about it, and he couldn't risk them getting hurt. Even with a half dozen part-time employees, there weren't quite enough watchful eyes to go around.

The employees he'd hoped to add this year needed to be reconsidered, just like everything else. Actually, Stuart thought, as he put a hand on his aching back and loaded one more tree on the trailer, he actually felt pretty blessed. Every single one of his part-time employees volunteered their time this year, none of them willing to accept pay. It would be a big help, even if he felt bad accepting it. Still, he was going to look at the bright side, and make sure they got a raise next year. He'd promised them that.

His phone chimed with the sound a voicemail left. Must be important, then. With a sigh, he took off his work gloves, tossed them onto the trailer, and picked up his phone.

The missed phone number wasn't one he recognized, but he punched the voicemail number and listened.

"Hello, this is Allison with your insurance company."

He winced. This was it. The final verdict. Maybe. How long did insurance things take, anyway? Weeks? This was his first time with anything like this.

"I just wanted you to know we got the fire marshal's report back."

Oh boy. This was it. He almost disconnected the call. It was too much to handle right now. His stomach churned like he'd eaten a bad burrito.

"And they have ruled this as an accidental fire. I need you to stop by the office so that I can have you sign a few things, and we can release a check to you as soon as possible. We are going to try and expedite the claim so that you can have your check in about a week."

There was silence on the line, but the call hadn't disconnected. Allison's voice, softer now, less business like, said, *"I'm...never mind. Just stop by at your earliest convenience."*

Then the call disconnected. Stuart wondered what she was about to say. Was there something wrong? Something she wasn't telling him? The tone of her voice had been so different. It had been...he wasn't sure. So far, Allison had only been professional. Annoyingly practical. It was obvious she didn't have a drop of Christmas cheer in her veins, but she'd been professional enough not to let that get in the way of helping him. This sounded almost...sympathetic? Kind?

Now he was imagining things. That woman wasn't either of those things. He checked his watch. It was close to five. There's no way the insurance office would still be open by the time he got cleaned up. He'd just go in the morning.

Stuart got back to work, making himself load another dozen trees before driving the trailer back to his house. Carl was going to take the trees to the chipper tomorrow, and the resulting pile of debris would become mulch, feeding the existing trees.

Dinner was spaghetti. A third of a box of noodles and plain jarred sauce to save money, with a slice of bread and margarine. He was so tired though, he did let himself have some iced tea to go with it, not just water.

His eyes catching the calendar on the wall, Stuart sighed. Days were ticking down and it was almost time to set up for his busiest weekend of the year. The women who usually sold their baked goods and jams had still planned to come, so at least there would be something for the customers, even if their choice of the perfect tree was slim.

Carl's idea of asking other tree farms for some of their stock didn't pan out. While all were willing to discount, it wasn't by much, and once he figured in the hauling fee to get the trees there, he would have been in the hole. He was already in one, so getting in another wasn't something he relished.

The stack of Christmas DVDs caught his eye. He was behind on those. Just wasn't feeling it this year. Was that what it was like to be Allison? Just never in the Christmas spirit?

The thought made him frown. He was already feeling the void that it left. How could a person not want that Christmas feeling at all? A shiver came over him then, and he stomped over, put in *It's a Wonderful Life*, and decided that wasn't going to happen to him. Things had taken a bad turn, sure. But things happened to others and they recovered, somehow. It just took perseverance. Grit. Determination. Faith.

Maybe, just like George Bailey, he'd get his Christmas spirit back. It was there, somewhere inside him, and he wasn't going to let anything or anyone take it away from him. Not the fire, not his situation, and not Allison.

CHAPTER 10

Allison clicked her pen. Then clicked it again. And again. She felt nervous. She wasn't exactly sure why. Then, someone paused in front of her office door and she felt her mouth go dry. It was Stuart. She studied him for a moment. He hadn't seen her yet. He was busy talking to a cluster of people who'd surrounded him.

When had the sight of him, or the mention of him, start her heart beating a little faster? And why did it? He was the complete opposite of her. Christmas incarnate. Not the sort of person she'd want to be friends with, let alone romantically tangled with.

And why was that even popping into her mind? She hardly knew the guy! Allison bit her lip and tried to focus on something other than his warm, rich voice. It was no good. Another person approached him, and she listened in.

"I appreciate it," he said. "No, I'm not giving up. Christmas is too important to all of us. Where there's a will, there's a way, and I'm working on it. I am grateful for your support more than you can know."

As his enthusiasm filled the small area he was in, Allison was surprised to see how relieved the people clustered around him looked. How happy. Radiant, even. Stuart looked the same. It was almost as if they all fed that energy to one another. What would that feel like? She felt surprisingly hollow.

When he finally waved goodbye to them and walked into her office, she put on her professional smile. "It's good to see you again," she said.

"Is it?" Stuart asked mildly as he met her gaze. "I get the impression you aren't a fan of Christmas anything, and by default, me."

She blinked several times. "That—that is—"

"No problem," he said, and eased into the chair, looking more comfortable than she'd seen him before. "I got your voicemail. What do I need to do?"

Allison nodded. "Right." Keep it business related. That was her job. That monetary lapse a moment ago was obviously the silliness of the season and that Hallmark movie she'd let Kenny talk her into seeing last night. It was all getting to her, and it was a wonder she was still coherent, and not decked out in red and green, singing songs. She pulled a folder toward herself. "I've printed out everything you'll need to sign. Once that's done, I'll get this processed and it will take about a week to be able to cut your check."

She removed the papers, set them before him, and leaned close, pointing out the different parts on the policy, aligning them to the column of numbers, and pointing where he needed to sign, initial, and sign again on each of the fourteen pages.

Stuart did so, and then asked, "Anything else?"

She shook her head. "No. That is, well, do you mind if I ask you a question?"

He looked surprised and set down the pen. "Sure. What?"

"Just a little bit ago, you were talking to others about your plans. What plans do you have for the farm? Were you able to find a way to save it? Salvage your Christmas sales?"

A tight expression flashed across his face. Just as quickly, it was gone, and instead he shrugged. "Between the two of us, I don't know yet. But I'm sure it will happen. Something will happen. I am going to do my best, because that's all I can do."

"I don't understand you," Allison said, the frustration bursting out of her. "After what happened, why do you want to do the same old thing? Why not do something different? Try a new thing?"

He frowned then, and she apologized. "I'm sorry. It's none of my business. I shouldn't be prying."

"No, it's fine," he answered. He was quiet a moment, then said, "Join me for a hot chocolate?

There's a place around the corner. My treat. No offense, but there are a lot of people hovering, and I'd rather not talk around all of them since I don't have a plan yet."

"Sure," she said, and stood.

The moment her purse was in her hand, she didn't know why she'd said yes. By the look of surprise on his face, she assumed he also didn't know why. Allison led the way through the office, to the glass front doors, and they stepped out onto the sidewalk. Her mother's excited expression flashed through her mind and she tried to blink it away.

It was nearing lunchtime, and her stomach growled. "How about lunch?" he asked.

"Sure," Allison said. "But that's my treat. Consider it a donation to keeping the tree farm going."

Again, she surprised herself, and him too she figured, by the hesitation, then nod coming from him. They walked around the corner to the small diner.

An older woman greeted them, and Stuart smiled at her. "Hello, Wilma," he said. "Table for two, please."

The woman led them to a table, dropped two menus and waited while they ordered cocoa, waters, Allison a chicken salad, and Stuart a grilled cheese with tomato and bacon.

As they waited for their food, Stuart said, "I've been coming to this place since I was a kid. I think Wilma's been here just as long. You have any traditions?"

Allison thought a moment. "Not really," she said.

He nodded slowly. "I wondered." Their food arrived and he dropped his napkin in his lap, took a bite, and after swallowing said, "You asked why I don't do something different. Well, I like traditions. I like the sameness. There's stability in it. Familiarity. I like those things."

"I do too," Allison said.

"Then why don't you like Christmas?" he asked her.

Allison frowned and twirled her fork around. "It's a long story."

"I can eat slow," he told her.

For some reason, that made her laugh. She shrugged, and a moment later said, "When I was a kid, I loved Christmas. All kids do, right?" At his nod, she continued, "It was going to be the best year ever. Dad had just gotten a raise, and there were more presents under the tree than we'd ever seen. We watched a Christmas movie before bed, left out cookies for Santa, and woke to the smell of smoke and the screeching of the smoke detector.

"The lights on the tree had faulty wiring, and caught our house on fire. The fire department came, and eventually got the fire out while my family stood outside watching. Neighbors were milling around, but no one was talking to us. No one was helping us. We were outside barefoot and cold and scared, and I kept thinking, this isn't right. It's Christmas. Aren't they supposed to help us? Or a miracle happen? But nothing did. No one did anything. It was like they couldn't be bothered.

"We got put in a cheap motel, and the first day back at school, when I didn't have my homework, my teacher made fun of me. She didn't care either. Didn't want to listen. Meanwhile, all my classmates kept talking about the great gifts they'd gotten for Christmas. The things they did. Other than a stuffed dog one of the firemen gave me, I didn't get any gifts. It sounds petty, I get it, and selfish, after all, we made it out alive, but I was a scared kid who had believed so much in Christmas and the idea of the miracle that would happen. When it didn't, it crushed me. I couldn't wait until all the Christmas talk was over, and I've never liked it since."

Allison didn't realize she'd started to cry until a rough thumb brushed away a tear. It startled her, and she dabbed at her face with her napkin.

"Sounds like that was a pretty difficult thing," Stuart said, his eyes filled with compassion. "I can see why Christmas would have bad memories attached. Working on my insurance case too. Christmas trees aren't really your favorite thing, and I understand why now."

Taking a deep breath, Allison tried to regain control of herself. She offered a weak smile. "It likely sounds stupid to you," she said. "No one was hurt, no one died."

"No," Stuart said, and then he surprised her. "But you lost something just as precious and important. Your sense of safety and security, and that stayed with you, and turned into an absolute dislike of anything that triggered that memory."

Allison nodded. "You are right. My parents bought us a few gifts later, wrapped them up too. But it wasn't the same, and seeing those gifts just made me remember everything all over."

At his sympathetic nod, Allison realized Stuart might be different from what she first thought. It made her want to know more about him. If this Christmas tree farm was his dream, something he was so passionate about, why wasn't he interested in trying something different?

"I get traditions are important to you," Allison said. "They are to a lot of people. But with the way things are right now, why don't you try something different?"

"What would I do?" Stuart asked. He held his hands out in a helpless gesture. "I'm one man. I have one employee who is full time, and a handful who help me seasonally. That's it. I don't have the manpower or the money for something different. Simple and small, it's all I can do."

"Well, you must have been planning something more before this happened," Allison said. "Can you still do any of those things?"

He shook his head. "I can't. They all take money. Something I don't have any of right now." He gave the last bite of grilled cheese a sad look. "I've cut back on everything, even been eating cheap. This might be the best thing I've eaten all week. I'm getting real tired of spaghetti and rice and beans, but you do what you have to do."

"That's why I don't understand why you don't try something different," Allison said.

Stuart looked at her and frowned. "Why do you care?" he asked. "You don't like Christmas or Christmas trees. Me...that's my whole world. My life revolves around them."

She shrugged then. His words stung, but she pressed on. "I guess just a part of me feels bad. For you, for the people who love going to your farm, and for the fact that it was likely something really simple that kept you from having the coverage that you needed."

He nodded, and gave her a crooked smile. "Maybe there's hope for you yet. A soft heart that beats beneath that Scrooge exterior."

"I doubt it," she joked.

Stuart looked into the distance. "I know some people can just distance themselves. Move on when they don't like things. That's not me though," he told her. "That's why I play it safe."

The check came then, interrupting them, and Stuart pulled out his wallet. "This one was on me," Allison said. "Remember?"

"This one," Stuart repeated. "Does that mean there might be another one, someday?"

CHAPTER 11

The question made her blush, and Stuart couldn't help but think she looked pretty cute with her cheeks all flushed. He felt comfortable around her, and liked that he could make jokes or tease her. She didn't seem to mind it either. He liked that she had a sense of humor.

For some reason, hearing her share that personal story made Allison seem more real, and less unapproachable. It also reminded him that not everyone did like Christmas, and some people have very valid reasons for it. You just might not know what it was. He felt a little bad for having been critical of her.

Stuart studied her as she raised her glass to buy time to answer. When his eyes didn't leave hers, she answered finally, "Maybe. People like you need people like me to keep them grounded." There was a smile playing on her lips.

He laughed then, a deep rich laugh that burst out of him and felt good to do. He'd been too gloomy as of late. "Is that so?" he asked. "If you ask me, people like you need people like me to help them find the magic in the world around them."

She frowned. "I don't need magic," she said. "Magic doesn't do anything for you."

Stuart shrugged. "You could be right. I don't know. I just know that I'm going to try my best to get through the next year."

"You could get a loan," she suggested. "Surely the banks would do that,"

He shook his head. "Nope. I'm not going to. Cash only. I am not going to finance, risk something happening, and lose my home because I have no way of paying it off."

"You are stubborn," Allison mused.

It was his turn to frown. "Well, I'm also someone who's been seeing how this business is done my whole life. Sometimes you have to be careful. Be choosy on what you do. Make sacrifices to help others or do the right thing."

The look on her face made him flash with anger suddenly. She looked at him like Molly had, when she'd told him to choose—her or the farm. She'd wanted him to sell the land too. Make a bundle. Traditions hadn't meant anything to her, either. Figures, he'd be dealing with that again.

When Allison didn't say anything, he said, a hint of heat in his voice, "You wouldn't understand. Women like you don't."

"What's that supposed to mean?" she asked, her jaw dropping. "I'm just trying to help."

"I don't need your pity," he said. "And I don't need your pressure to do something that is going to hurt the tree farm in some way."

Allison's eyes widened. "I wasn't—"

"It's okay," he said, and stood up. "I appreciate the lunch. Appreciate getting to know you a little better. But when it comes to my business, I need to do what I think is best."

"You're right," she said, her eyes lowered. "I'm sorry. I just...wanted to make some suggestions. Maybe help."

"I don't get that," Stuart said. He shook his head as she slid out of the booth and started to the door.

"Why?" Allison pushed the door open and stepped onto the sidewalk.

"Because I don't know why you care. This is your job. You've made your dislike of my business abundantly clear."

Allison looked like she was going to defend herself, but he held out a hand to stop her. "Know what's crazy? When I first saw you, something about you...I don't know. I wanted to know you better. I wanted to bring a smile to your face. Hearing your story today, I wanted to help you find the magic of Christmas that was obviously missing from you. To show you that life has wonder all around and good people in it.

"But I don't think you'll ever let anyone do it. You keep saying I should do something different, but I sure don't see you doing or talking about doing different for yourself. You avoid what you don't like." He laughed then, almost bitterly. "Guess we both are stuck in the past."

He took a last look at her. "I was in love once. About to propose. But she didn't want me for me. She wanted me for what she thought I could give her, by taking a loan. By selling the farm. I won't do that. Not for anyone. I'm going to make sure this Christmas is a good one at the tree farm, one way or another, and I'll do it without risking something more happening to the farm. I don't expect you to understand that, but I sure hope you'll have a good Christmas, Allison.

"You deserve one. You deserve presents under the tree, happy memories, and a lifetime of love. Those things are missing from your life, and it shows." He couldn't say anything else. There was nothing left to say. She just didn't understand how he felt, and he didn't know why, for just a moment, he'd thought she might.

She was staring at him, her mouth open. He refused to feel guilty, though. He was done. There were too many people who didn't understand how important the Christmas tree farm and Christmas itself was. He didn't have time to waste explaining to yet another person.

Stuart left then, and headed back to his farm. On the drive, he kept asking himself why he'd said that. He also wondered how his boastful words, words of making this a good Christmas, could come true.

Maybe he should have given her a chance. She wasn't Molly. He had to remember that. But he also didn't know her and she didn't know him.

He let out a long sigh. He'd probably been too harsh. Allison had only been trying to help. Her suggestions had been practical. Normal, even. But no, he couldn't do it.

He also couldn't get her face out of his mind. As he'd walked off, it was the hardest thing he'd ever had to do. She looked to small, so vulnerable. All he'd wanted to do was gather her into his arms and do whatever he could to help heal her broken heart, while healing his own.

Too bad she was right. Miracles just didn't happen.

Chapter 12

Allison walked through the door and fell onto the sofa. She was glad Kenny wasn't there. Stuart's words had cut her deeply. She'd just been trying to help. For a moment, she'd gotten caught up. Swayed, by the emotions of everyone around her about the Christmas tree farm.

And him. Allison had to admit that she was curious about Stuart. That drive and determination he had. She wanted to see him succeed. That's all, she told herself. That's the only reason she had wanted to help.

It wasn't at all because she felt just a tiny bit attracted to him. No way. Not at all. Well, maybe just a little. But not really.

She flopped her head back and sighed again. Picking up the remote, she flicked through channels to find something to distract her.

"Hot sale now! Get your Christmas list—"

Click.

"—for the perfect gift? Wow her this year—"

Click.

"But Mommy, we always make cookies for Christmas. I don't want to make a pie."

Click.

"Ho! Ho! H—"

Click.

Allison turned the TV off. Christmas. Everywhere. And it was just days before Thanksgiving. Why did people have to spend almost two months getting ready for a single day? The mail on the small table by the door caught her attention and she walked over and flipped through it.

Christmas sales. Christmas sweaters. Christmas trips. Christmas, Christmas, everywhere. She almost felt relief seeing her credit card bill. Almost.

Kenny walked in then, grinning at her. "What up, Scrooge?"

"Stop, please," she said. "Not today."

He frowned then. "What's wrong?"

Allison shook her head. "I don't know. I'm just tired of everyone calling me that. Tired of not being taken seriously, or when I offer help, someone acting like I've got an alternative agenda."

"What's this about?" he asked her, crossing his arms. "Someone upset you? Who can I take out for you? A few clicks and I can send a virus their way."

"Ugh. The tree farm guy. I asked him why didn't he try something different this year. I mean, everyone's been going around talking about how important and special the tree farm is, how it's tradition. He does too. But, it's pretty obvious to me that he needs to do something different this year if he's going to be able to do those things."

"Do what things?" Kenny asked.

"Make Christmas amazing," Allison said with a frown. "Let everyone have their happiness and traditions and all that stuff."

"And you think you can help?"

Her eyes shot to Kenny. There was no judgment there, only curiosity. "I don't know. I had this crazy idea..."

"Go on."

"It's stupid."

"Probably. But tell me anyway. It might not be. Could be one of those Christmas miracles things." Kenny wiggled his eyebrows up and down and Allison couldn't help but laugh.

"Okay. I was thinking of a way that he could not only keep the crowd, but also maybe draw in a larger one." Allison reached for some paper, and started making a basic sketch of the idea that had been floating around in her mind. "Look at this."

Half an hour later, Kenny sat back. "Al, this is brilliant. Like, amazing. Christmas miracle on TV kinda thing. You've got to tell him."

"I don't think he wants to talk to me anymore," she admitted.

"Doesn't matter. You need to tell him this. Seriously. It's not just for him. It's for everyone. For you."

"For me?" Allison felt surprised. "What do you mean?"

"I mean," Kenny said, and took up her hands in a squeeze, "you have had the most incredible idea. And more than that, being around this guy seems to have planted a tiny spark of Christmas in you. The spark you used to be filled with. I really miss that. Your giddy laughter, the over-the-top decorating. The stacks of movies you'd watch each season, and the eleven thousand cookies you made."

Allison shook her head and gave a dry laugh. "I don't have a spark of anything," she said.

"You do," he insisted. "And it's not a bad thing. It's good. Come on, I'll drive you."

"Drive me where?" she asked.

"Pressman's. You're going to tell him your idea."

"And you are coming because…"

"If he says no," Kenny said, jumping up and opening the front door, "I'm going to punch him. And steal his phone and put a virus on it. I also want to see this guy for myself. Since you like him and all."

"I don't like him," Allison protested as she moved through the door.

"Uh huh," Kenny said, locking it behind them.

"I still don't know," Allison said a moment later, snapping on her seatbelt.

"It's going to be okay," Kenny said. "I'll be there. I'm not going to let him snap at you."

"I'm not worried about that," Allison said, as the car pulled onto the two-lane highway.

Kenny shot her a glance. She turned to look out of the window to avoid his piercing look. He turned up the radio and began singing slightly off key.

Signs caught her eye and she read each one as they passed.

Jam and jelly. Freshly baked rolls. Local honey. Mark's Market, fresh milk daily.

"Am I doing the right thing?" she asked, to no one in particular. "I just need a sign."

"There's one," Kenny said, pointing.

Allison blinked in disbelief. A large sign had appeared in front of them, reading *Christmas is a time for miracles*.

"Well, that's a little too much of a coincidence," she said dryly.

Another sign appeared. *Just believe*.

"Okay, this is spooky," Allison said. She closed her eyes. "I'm not opening my eyes until we get there."

"Good thing I'm driving then," Kenny said. "This would have been a pretty dangerous drive. Imagine the bad press the company would get."

She laughed, and a moment later felt the crunching of gravel beneath the tires. She peeked through her eyelids, then opened them wider.

They were there. Stuart was standing near his truck, and there was a frown as he caught sight of her. He crossed his arms, leaned against the side of his truck, and waited while she and Kenny got out. His expression wasn't one of welcome at all, and Allison felt her stomach start to squeeze with nervousness.

Kenny took the lead. Allison still wasn't sure why he came, but she was grateful. "Hello, Kenny Jackson," he said, introducing himself. "Scrooge is my sister."

"Kenny," she hissed.

Her cheeks flamed, but to her surprise Stuart laughed. "Scrooge, huh? I thought that was my nickname for her."

"What?" Her head snapped up as her jaw opened.

"I like you already," Kenny said. Then he crossed his own arms. "Al told me she had a good idea. But she also told me she messed up trying to tell you about it. She does that. A lot. I should know. Personally, I care about this place. We came when we were kids, and I'm a sucker for a happy ending, so I am asking that you just listen to her idea."

"Is that so?" Stuart's eyes flickered over her. He glanced back at Kenny. "You two don't seem very much alike."

"When Al lost her Christmas cheer, I tried to absorb as much of it as I could, so it didn't go to waste," Kenny said with a grin. Then his face grew serious. "Really. I think you ought to listen."

Stuart nodded. "Alright then. I'm listening."

Allison wet her lips nervously. Her heart was hammering and she felt lightheaded. "Ah, that is," she started.

Kenny came to her rescue again, against Stuart's sharp gaze. "Can we go to the lot where it all happens?" he asked. "Then she can explain better."

"Sure," Stuart said. Allison wasn't sure what Kenny had asked, but it seemed Stuart did. "Was just about to haul these tables out there for the ladies who set up jam."

"Perfect," Kenny said. He jumped in the back of the truck. "We'll help you unload."

Stuart nodded, looking uncertain, but then walked around and held the passenger door open for Allison. She climbed in and closed the door as he slid himself into the driver's seat.

As the engine turned over and he put it into gear, he said, "Didn't think I'd see you anytime soon."

"I wanted to tell you I'm sorry. Sorry for everything. Most of all, sorry for you thinking I was trying to force an idea on you that you wouldn't like. I know you may not believe it, but over the last few days I've been thinking a lot, and I see how important this place is—to you and the town."

"That's when you came up with this idea, huh?" he asked. He shot her a look then. "I'm sorry too. I overreacted. Said things I didn't mean. This place means a lot to me though. So do the people in the town."

"I see that," Allison said. "Let bygones be bygones?" She held out a hand and he shook it.

"Agreed." He checked his rearview mirror and laughed. "Your brother looks like a pup riding in the back."

Allison turned behind her and joined in his laughter. It was true. Kenny had his chin pointed up and his nose in the air with his eyes closed. "I let him out, but he's housebroken," she said.

Stuart chuckled then, and some of the tension she'd felt in the air seemed to melt. "Go on then," he said. "What were you saying?"

Allison took a deep breath. "I was saying that I was sorry. That you were right, and I wasn't, when I suggested a loan or selling the place. The more I listened, really listened to what you and others were saying, the more I realized that while this is your business, it's more than that. You help others. Like a modern day Santa."

He looked at her sideways, then focused back on the road. They were driving slowly, but would be there soon.

"I heard about what you do, other than just growing trees," she pressed on, wanting to get her apology out entirely before they stopped and Kenny was there with her. "The kids that you buy gifts for in the women's shelter. How you treated all the police and firefighters and rescue squad volunteers to a dinner. Donated a tree and then a gift to each person at the senior home."

Stuart squirmed in the seat. "No one's supposed to know about that," he said, his voice gruff. "How'd you hear about it?"

Allison smiled. "You aren't as sneaky as you think," she teased, then reached out and rested her hand on his. They'd pulled up and were waiting to get out.

A warm tingle ran through her fingertips, and based on the way he looked down at her hand, he felt it too. Stuart looked at her. His eyes searched her face for a long moment. "That's part of why I need sales to be good this year," he said. "A lot of people depend on me."

"And that's why I have an idea," she whispered. "You do so much for others to help them. Will you please let me help you?"

CHAPTER 13

Stuart stood, hands on his hips. Two children ran past, giggling and holding candy canes that Santa had just given them. Everywhere he looked, it was Christmas. Over the top, larger than life, Christmas.

He had to admit, Allison's idea was incredible. Everyone in town thought so too. Somehow, she, along with her brother and Carl, had pulled off a miracle.

Someone stood next to him, and he saw it was Allison, holding two paper cups. She offered one, and then smiled up at him. "It's better than I imagined," she said, her eyes taking in the field.

Stuart followed her gaze. Thousands of Christmas lights were strung up, creating a beautiful glow as dusk came. Christmas music was playing, provided by a mixture of the high school orchestra, the local fire department, and some seniors on brass, who really added a lot with their experience.

A half dozen food trucks were parked, and families crowded the windows, then sat with their orders at picnic tables spread around. Trees, freshly cut, were browsed while some families went to the field holding a small stake with their name and information on it to "adopt" a tree that they could collect seven years from now.

There were local craftspeople, a story time for children put on by the local library, and of course the Santa, whose large belly shook wildly with each ho, ho, ho.

A station was set up where volunteers assisted in painting ornaments created out of the trunks of the charred trees they could salvage. The tractor, filled with hay and singing voices, drove past and Stuart waved at Kenny, who was on it and singing at the top of his lungs, slightly off key.

Local businesses had donated items, faster than he'd thought possible, and a silent auction had been created, with all proceeds going to the replanting of the farm and the following year's operating expenses.

It wasn't just a simple Christmas tree farm anymore. It had become a half day of entertainment for families to come out and enjoy.

More than that, it had become a real Christmas miracle.

"What do you think?" Allison asked.

"It's different," Stuart said. Then he put his cup down and took hers out of her hand, setting it next to his. "But different isn't bad. Even if things aren't the same as they used to be, it's about it's about coming together with a new idea that makes everything right. It's the start of a new tradition."

"Is that so?" she said, looking up at him.

He couldn't resist the smile on her face, and leaned in closer. "That's right," he said. "And I'd like to start a new tradition, one with you."

"What's that?" Allison asked.

Her eyes were wide, and in the soft glow of the Christmas lights, he wanted nothing more to kiss her. Hesitation gripped at him, but he pressed forward. "I'd like to spend next Christmas season with you, just like this," he said. "Maybe all the ones afterward?"

Her arms slid around his waist, and the electric current from them filled him. "Just Christmas?" she asked.

"And New Year. Valentines. All times. Every day. Every night. Each moment." He held his breath.

"Is this your way of asking me out?" Allison teased.

"Yes," Stuart said. "Will you go out with me? You can pick what we do."

Allison smiled at him then, and rose to her tiptoes. As her lips met his, he thought nothing had ever felt so perfect. There was a palatable loss when she broke away.

"How about dinner and a movie?" she asked.

"Sounds good," Stuart agreed. Though, he would have agreed to anything she wanted. "What movie?"

"Anything Christmas," Allison said, threading her fingers though his. "They're my favorite type, you know. I have a lot of them to get caught up on."

Stuart smiled and wrapped his arm around her. As Allison rested her head on his shoulder, he couldn't help but feel the warmth of the Christmas spirit filling him.

What could have been a tragedy turned into something incredible. "Guess I got that miracle after all," he mumbled, holding his cocoa to his lips.

When Allison turned to smile at him again, he knew without a doubt it was true. And it might have taken a while, but it appeared Allison had gotten one too.

The moon lit the sky, and it started to snow. White flakes drifted down, and everyone there laughed and gasped, with many of the children and adults spinning around to catch flakes. Kenny drove past them again, this time driving the tractor while waving one arm and shouting, "Merry Christmas to all! And to all, a good night!"

Stuart called back, his arms tightly around Allison, "And God bless us, every one."

Note from Author

Thank you for taking the time to read this book, *No Insurance for a Miracle*.

Could I ask for one small favor? Reviews like yours on Amazon mean so much to me and help others to find my books! Even just a single line means a lot!

WANT A **FREE** BOOK?

Stop by my website to get your no strings attached **FREE book**. It's my gift to you, as a thank you for reading this book.

www.sarahlambbooks.com

Ready for more?

Want more of my books? I write for children and adults!

Find them all on Amazon here:

https://www.amazon.com/stores/Sarah-Lamb/author/B098H3SGLK

And all current Small Town Christmas series books here:

https://www.amazon.com/dp/B0DTF8Q225

ABOUT THE AUTHOR

Sarah writes captivating characters and clean romance that's anything BUT boring! From heartbreaking moments to heartwarming tales, get swept away in either historical or small town romance that pulls you in until the last page.

Nestled in the Blue Ridge Mountains of Virginia where she's married to her Texan husband, you'll find Sarah creating her next book, homeschooling her two boys, or volunteering in her community.

Want more of Sarah's books? Find them all on Amazon!

https://www.amazon.com/stores/Sarah-Lamb/author/B098H3SGLK